Lyle Walks the Dogs

A COUNTING BOOK

By BERNARD WABER   Illustrated by PAULIS WABER

Houghton Mifflin Books for Children

HOUGHTON MIFFLIN HARCOURT

BOSTON NEW YORK

For Paulis,
again with love.
Qvell, qvell!
—B.W.

For my father, whose kindness,
humor, wisdom, and friendship
have blessed each day of my life.
—P.W.

Text copyright © 2010 by Bernard Waber
Illustrations copyright © 2010 by Paulis Waber

All rights reserved. For information about permission to reproduce selections from this book, write to
Permissions, Houghton Mifflin Harcourt Publishing Company, 215 Park Avenue South, New York, New York 10003.

Houghton Mifflin Books for Children is an imprint of Houghton Mifflin Harcourt Publishing Company.

www.hmhbooks.com

The text of this book is set in Scala.
The illustrations are watercolor, ink and pencil.

Library of Congress Cataloging-in-Publication Control Number 2009032047

ISBN 978-0-547-22323-0

Printed in Singapore
TWP 10 9 8 7 6 5 4 3 2
4500237971

Lyle the Crocodile has a job, a brand-new job.

Lyle's job is walking dogs.

It is a very good job for Lyle because Lyle loves dogs.

And he loves to walk.

And best of all, Lyle loves being helpful to others.

Lyle is so happy. Today is Day 1, the first day of his job.

1

GWENDOLYN

DAY 1

Lyle walks **1** dog.

The dog's name is Gwendolyn.

Uh-oh! Gwendolyn is frisky.

She pulls this way and she pulls that way.

Lyle must take quick skipping steps to keep up with Gwendolyn.

No problem. Lyle loves skipping.

DAY 2

Lyle walks **2** dogs.

Count them—**1-2.** The second dog's name is Morris.

Oh . . . and guess what?

Morris is even friskier.

Lyle must take even quicker steps to keep up
with Morris.

No more skipping. Too bad!

3

POKEY

DAY 3

Lyle walks **3** dogs.

Count them—**1-2-3.**

The third dog's name is Pokey.

Pokey takes his own good,

sweet time walking.

Slow down, Morris!
Slow down, Gwendolyn!
Come along, Pokey!
Good going, Pokey.
Good work, Lyle.

4

FRISKY

DAY 4

Lyle walks **4** dogs.
Count them—**1-2-3-4.**
The fourth dog's name is . . .
oh, no! Her name is Frisky.
Hang on to Frisky, Lyle!

DAY 5

Lyle walks **5** dogs.

Count them—**1-2-3-4-5.**

The fifth dog's name is Rosie.

Rosie loves birds, bugs, flowers, children—
and Lyle. Most certainly Lyle.

6

SNAPPY

DAY 6

Business is picking up.

Lyle walks **6** dogs.

Count them—**1-2-3-4-5-6.**

The sixth dog's name is Snappy.

Snappy is . . . well . . . rather snappish.

He barks and barks. And barking, as you know, can be quite contagious, especially for dogs.

Six dogs barking. What a racket! What to do?

Leave it to Lyle.

His gentle tugs, pats, and shushes calm everyone—

even snappish Snappy.

7

TULIP

DAY 7

Lyle's excellent reputation for walking dogs has spread.

Lyle walks **7** dogs. Count them—**1-2-3-4-5-6-7.**

The seventh dog's name is Tulip.

Tulip had to be coaxed out from under the couch.

Everyone waited and waited for her.

But now look at Tulip.
Just look at her trotting along,
merrily wagging her tail with the best of them.

8

SCRAPPY

DAY 8

Lyle walks **8** dogs.

Count them—**1-2-3-4-5-6-7-8**.

The eighth dog's name is Scrappy.

Scrappy runs, stops, or sits as he

chooses to run, stop . . .

. . . or sit.

There's trouble on East 88th Street.

Grrrr

Grrrr

Woof!

Snarl, snarl!

Arf!

Not to worry. Lyle is on the job.
His kind heart and big croc smile win the day.
Scrappy falls quickly in step,
and all step cheerfully together.
Big cheers for Lyle.

9

RUFUS

DAY 9

Lyle walks **9** dogs.

Count them—**1-2-3-4-5-6-7-8-9.**

The ninth dog's name is Rufus.

Rufus is so happy to be walking with Lyle.

He scratched at his window for days, yearning to join the walk.

And Lyle is tickled to have Rufus aboard.

10

SNIFFY

DAY 10

Lyle walks **10** dogs.

Count them—**1-2-3-4-5-6-7-8-9-10.**

The tenth dog's name is Sniffy.

Sniffy walks nose to the ground,
sniffing, sniffing, sniffing.

Suddenly, Sniffy is on to something.
What?

FISH

BAGELS

FLOWERS

A SQUIRREL!

The dogs run.
The squirrel runs
Lyle runs, too.

Are all of the dogs here?

Let's count them and see.

1

GWENDOLYN

2

MORRIS

3

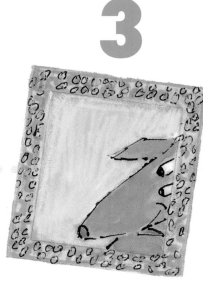

POKEY

7

TULIP

8

SCRAPPY

9

RUFUS

4

FRISKY

5

ROSIE

6

SNAPPY

10

SNIFFY

They are all here.

Safe, well—and thirsty.
Good dogs!

And—

Good job, Lyle!